Beyond the Veil

Beyond the Veil

Enter the Temple, Enter Heaven

By
C. N. DUDEK

RESOURCE *Publications* · Eugene, Oregon

BEYOND THE VEIL
Enter the Temple, Enter Heaven

Resource Publications
An Imprint of Wipf and Stock Publishers
199 W. 8th Ave., Suite 3
Eugene, OR 97401

www.wipfandstock.com

PAPERBACK ISBN 13: 978-1-4982-8244-4
HARDCOVER ISBN 13: 978-1-4982-8246-8

Manufactured in the U.S.A.   03/18/2016

To Sara
And to my friends

"Use?" replied Reepicheep. "Use, Captain? If by use you mean filling our bellies or our purses, I confess it will be no use at all. So far as I know we did not set sail to look for things useful but to seek honour and adventure."

–C. S. Lewis, *The Voyage of the Dawn Treader*

"Dead men cannot take effective action; their power of influence on others lasts only till the grave. Deeds and actions that energise others belong only to the living."

–St. Athanasius, *On the Incarnation*

Contents

Chapter 1 | 1

Chapter 2 | 4

Chapter 3 | 7

Chapter 4 | 11

Chapter 5 | 18

Chapter 6 | 23

Chapter 7 | 27

Chapter 8 | 31

Chapter 9 | 36

Chapter 10 | 40

Chapter 11 | 45

Chapter 12 | 52

Appendix | 57

Chapter 1

The moon slipped behind a cumulus sailing across dark skies. It was a balmy night, early fall. Fall bringing a season of contemplation after a burning summer, draining creativity. Crisp fall clears the mind as nights get cooler and time settles before stopping in frozen winter-scape.

At least this is how Nicholas Ignatius saw the world. He had just closed shop, books in hand, pining to amble the orange-lamped sidewalks embracing cooler evenings and clearer thought.

Nicholas breathed in chilled air contemplating; taking in the view of row homes on either side, passing the post office, the willow over the rambling creek. How the homes sat silently as petrified giants awaiting the trumpet to awake them and ruin the town. Passing Oak Street where oaks used to stand like pillars, holding the ground in place, supporting the sky. But now, those ancient sentinels, torn from the supple ground where a housing development would take their place.

Passing Westmoreland Street, he remembered his friend Tom, where they used to play catch in his backyard. Tom's father had died when he was fifteen; the house sold, the family uprooted, a friend gone; last Nicholas heard, Tom went off to war and hadn't heard anything since. On to Green walking through Belle Grove Park, remembering holding hands with his first love, his first kiss, near the fountain.

Nicholas sat on a park bench facing Bond Street. The houses still, windows dark. The homes had been there since the thirties. How many families had lived there over the years? How many dead and gone?

This night in November marked the second anniversary of Nicholas' father's death. He remembered the requiem mass. Paschal candle burning—the presence of Jesus Christ, his eternal kingdom just beyond the veil. The tears, the sorrow, the solemnity. The saturnine presence with virulent life juxtaposed.

This was a difficult time in Nicholas' life—the most difficult. Not making that initiation leap with his father's blessing had torn him from certainty—how to function in this broken world. Fear, anxiety, hatred of self, all posed as daggers eviscerating his marriage to his lovely wife. The pain of the past melding with the present had left their marriage a tattered sail torn by the winds, rains, storms of broken psyche, wayward self-deprecating habits. What was once a beautiful sail filled with winds journeying this couple toward adventure and life, was now unrecognizable—a tattered, threadbare unity, now disparate.

As Nicholas thought of his life, a ruin, a long forgotten relic, he wandered the streets in no particular direction. The moon sat high in the balmy atmosphere—shining moonbeams. Jupiter, Mars, and Venus all lingered in the sky making a beautiful pointed, dazzling trinity. He thought of the medieval man walking in days of old—looking to the sky as the heavens filled with daemons, angels, unseen creatures of God's cosmos. Nicholas loathed the modern view of space—the word "space" alone vexed him. The heavens are not just vacuous meaningless space. As Nicholas ambled down Windsor Drive he thought of the beauty of the cosmos. Yet a doubt lingered in him—was all this matter meaningless? Or is all there is, matter alone?

He stopped. A red door lit by artificial light stood in the distance. A door once familiar to him. He walked down the drive and pulled on the door, luckily it was unlocked. He entered.

The sanctuary was dimly lit, the eternal candle burning above the tabernacle in its red sconce. Nicholas recalled something an orthodox priest once told him, "Once you enter the church; you enter heaven." He sat contemplating, thinking, taking in the images surrounding him. The crucifix hanging in the present, yet making present that Good Friday. Head bowed, eyes closed, he prayed, something he hadn't done for years, uncertain what to say, "Lord, help me, Lord have mercy." With eyes closed, Nicholas wept in agony. Mourning his marriage, mourning all that was lost: his father, his joy, his peace. A red hue dominated the room.

The penitent felt a crushing, as though the atmosphere was compressed; he at the center of a vice. The pressure then subsided. He felt a peace as though a spring rain washed over him or the peace and reinvigoration of a rest on vacation.

Something indescribable changed. Nicholas rose to his feet. He walked to the door and opened it to a twilit sky of red—facing west. The moon was rising, seemingly larger than he'd ever seen before.

But what struck him was he could see Venus in the sky, the way one can see the moon during daylight hours—a white disc in the sky. In fact, he could see many of the other planets: Mercury, Mars, Saturn, and most prominent Jupiter.

The air was cleaner—he breathed in deeply feeling refreshed unlike the usual air he was used to.

"Have I been transported somewhere? Did I fall asleep in the chapel?" Nicholas said in a whisper.

He had always dreamed of a time without combustion, electricity, without a care in the world. With only the soft sounds of wind, trees, animal sounds, maybe a carriage creaking down a dirt road. In fact, none of the usual sounds of motor cars were heard. Buildings, sidewalk, road disappeared. Yet, the chapel still stood behind him.

"Where am I?"

Chapter 2

"At the culmination of time," a voice said.

Nicholas turned. A man stood there. Nicholas saw a man, but there was something more to him than mere flesh, Nicholas could only think of the word *gravitas*. The man was an embodiment of that word.

"Who are you?"

"I am Rigel. I was told to come to your aid, and so I have."

"Rigel . . . Who told you?"

"Why, the king of this place of course. And yes, you do recognize my name correctly. I am he."

Nicholas had studied astronomy as a novice for many years. He would gaze into the heavens pointing out the constellations, finding the stars he knew by name. Rigel was one of them. The foot of Orion.

"I have always dreamed that stars would be more than what they were made of. Their unseen being a true reality. How wonderful to meet you," Nicholas said. "Who is the king of this place? I would think someone numinous and benevolent or a great tyrant. But I don't think this world seems oppressed, though I have only been here quite brief."

"You would be correct that this king is other, but he is not a tyrant, yet to be feared as one is in awe of majesty. But come, let us explore what your heart seeks: truth, healing, life, peace, and love."

Chapter 2

Rigel led Nicholas upon a rolling hill of green. The breeze swept across the fields, swaying the green like wind on water, changing hues, a dazzling to the eye. The sun was warm, yet Nicholas looked to the sky and saw no solar disc, yet light lit the land, but somehow the light was luminous and soothing, the way a lazy afternoon feels, restful, at ease, having no particular place to be, content. Nicholas could only dredge up feelings to describe what he saw.

They traveled through the fields of green to a wooded glade where beeches and pine trees stood in rows. As Nicholas walked through the woods, images and feelings of his childhood swept through his imagination. A place of serenity, of peace, of joy. Nicholas' heart was about to burst in joy, he almost felt like weeping. He looked at each tree in wonder, at each fern that grew. At the pine needles that blanketed the ground. His eyes were opened to a childlike wonder that he had long forgotten. The silence was a balm to his soul, yet not empty. The silence was pregnant with hope, joy, something Nicholas could not fully describe.

As they continued walking, they came upon a man kneeling amongst the trees and light, his eyes closed; a smile on his face.

"What is this man doing? Is he okay?" Nicholas said.

"He is. In his life, he never had a second to spare to enjoy the created natural beauty surrounding him. He has chosen to spend some amount of time to satisfy this deficiency within him. Then he will move on and journey further in, reaching his destination. Just as you must," said Rigel.

"Is this paradise but a staging point?"

"In a way, yes. There is much within you that must be healed, that you must let go of," Rigel said.

"Purgation, huh," said Nicholas.

With that Rigel smiled and turned. "Come, over this hill, we reach the first stage. Let us go swiftly." Rigel started running, almost gliding, dancing over the ferns and pine needles. The trees swayed toward him in his wake. Nicholas ran too. He felt light. As though a burden had been lifted. He ran, much like in a dream, without fatigue, without heaviness of breath.

They ran for what seemed several miles, stopping at a breathtaking scene. Below them lay a valley covered in mist, a stream running through it. Nicholas traced the stream with his eye upward, all the way to a mountainside that stood what seemed miles high. A rushing waterfall crashed over its side.

"We must climb the mountain, my friend," Rigel said. "It will not be easy, but it will transform you." With that, Rigel ran ahead; Nicholas following.

Chapter 3

Nicholas followed Rigel down the hillside and through a lush, green valley. The river always near them. They followed it as though it was a road. They ascended as the river descended. They reached the foot of the mountain where a large pool of water lay.

Nicholas dove into the water. He expected cold mountain water, but it was warm and seemed heavier than water. As he swam through the pool, his spirits lifted, an energy thrilled through him. He had not experienced this kind of thing since he had first known there was more to the world than just plain matter. When he realized there were deeper, richer, numinous things in the world. That there was a being out there, yet closer than his own beating heart who loved every created thing. This joy, which he had not felt in years surged through him.

Nicholas burst through the surface of the water as though reborn. All he could do was smile. He could not articulate anything that he was feeling.

"Thrilling isn't it?" Rigel said. "There is much, much more of this to be known, to be experienced. Your heart, mind, spirit, your very being will transform as you journey. Some of the journey will be glorious, some will be difficult, and some will be near impossible."

"This water . . . or whatever it is . . . is seething with life. I feel refreshed. Like that of a cold wintry waste, where all is frozen, and by Jove, a sulfur spring is bubbling nearby. Its warmth from the depth of the earth thawing the rigid, hardened soul within. This is similar, yet much more. Oh God, have I been dulled and deadened. Lord, thaw my frozen heart," Nicholas said.

"Come, this is only a quick energizing, there is more to do," Rigel said.

Nicholas waded to the shore. He stepped out of the water and followed Rigel up the narrow steep trail that worked its way up the mountain.

When they reached the top of the mountainside, there was a plateau. It was pitch black except for the stars. Nicholas could see billions of stars, the Milky Way, and more than he could have ever dreamed. It was more magnificent than a dark night sky dome in Colorado without a light for hundreds of miles.

"A shooting star," Nicholas shouted. He traced it across the sky. Off in the distance, a blinding white explosion razed his eyes. "What was that?"

"You must go and see. But you may not like what you see. It is blinding, beautiful, terrible, wondrous, filled with truth. It will tell you things you've always wanted to know; things you are ashamed of, things you must know, but wish not to," Rigel said.

Nicholas' hair stood on the back of his neck. He did not want to go out into the darkness alone. Yet he knew he must. "Will you come with me?"

Rigel shook his head. "No. But I will not be far behind. When you return, your burden will be lightened."

Nicholas slowly shuffled away into the unknown. Rigel gave Nicholas a firm, but gentle push, which compelled Nicholas to slowly jog which turned into a dash toward the distant white glow ahead.

When he reached the spot where the object fell to the ground, Nicholas could not see much besides a blinding white. He felt compelled to speak, "Hello."

What happened next is difficult to describe. All at once, Nicholas had millions of images of his life flash in his mind's eye. A voice spoke one word for each image: birth, life, grief, death, lust, peace, sin, anger, hatred, dread, despair, depression, fear, covetous, pain, rebirth, thanksgiving, suffering, death, resurrection, long-ing, yearning, joy, faith, hope, love . . . Millions of images, millions of words. Yet all within seconds. When this ended, Nicholas was dizzy, his brain overwhelmed. He had to lie down. Then a voice spoke, powerful, awful, but it was something good (which Nicho-las sensed):

"You have lied with the great deceiver. Fear, despair, pain, suf-fering has crowded your psyche. You have fallen upon swords of defeat. You lie close to the life-giving water, but you cannot see it or hear it babbling just over the hill. Much of you lay dormant, waiting. Fear paralyzing you. He wishes you to be set free. Your chains are heavy. His yoke is light. The King speaks peace, joy, life. He delights in you. You are the work of his hands. He is peace, joy, love, life."

Nicholas trembled as a child before a great beast, his words feeble and weak, "Are you this King Rigel speaks of?"

"No, I am but a servant."

"A great servant. You must be the one who sits at his right side—" Nicholas was cut short.

"Silence. Only one sits at his right side. You speak near blas-phemy . . . Forgive me, I have frightened you. I forget you still exist in weakness—your body has not been transformed. His message is: be set free, be transformed. I have been sent to burn away the flax, if you will. To rid you of some of the dross. You must speak, telling me all of your faults, then you will be cleansed, your lips, tongue, and hands purified."

Nicholas turned red. Heat and blood rising to his head. "I have not told anyone any of the things I have done wrong, not since childhood when I went to confession. I only tell my faults to God . . . maybe my wife."

The white light sighed . . . or what sounded like sighing. Nicholas did not know if this creature breathed at all. "I am the light of the evenstar. I am that which shines by day and by night. I hold all the words ever spoken. When spoken they are put to ac-tion or they are discarded never to be known by the King because he is ever merciful. Once these sins, these faults are voiced, they are put into the vessel of Lethe (of forgetfulness), the King pardons the one confessing. The confessor's burden lightened. The confessor is set free."

"Rigel did tell me I would not like what was to happen here. But you and he have told me this weight upon my heart would be lessened. I trust you. I know I do. The numinous is to be feared and respected. I will do as you tell me," Nicholas said.

Nicholas told the white light, or Evenstar, every sin he had committed since childhood—all he could remember. As he spoke, Nicholas felt different. The beginning of his unburdening. He told of his relationship with his wife—how it had gone sour. A lot because of him and his attitude, the way he saw his wife. His covetousness toward other women. Many things were spoken. As he spoke, his words manifested as bluish vapors coming from his mouth. Nicholas could see, faintly, a crystal flask and his words, now vapors, were collected within.

When Nicholas finished speaking, the flask was thrust to the ground; shattering into fragmented, refracted light, like diamonds bursting.

"Now come closer," Evenstar said.

Nicholas walked closer. He felt something firmly, yet gently grab his chin and pulled him forward. "From henceforth, your lips are cleansed, tongue purified, sins forgotten and forgiven in the name of the King."

At that, a bright yellow orb touched his lips. He was blinded by the intruding light and winced at the intense heat of the orb. His lips and tongue burned almost to the point of the sense of freezing temperatures. Nicholas shouted the intensity was so great. Yet, immediately, the sensation ceased, the orb gone, the white light gone—Evenstar gone.

Nicholas fell to his knees and wept. He was not in pain. In fact, all was well. He was filled with joy once again. "I am undone. I am a broken man."

Chapter 4

Rigel stood behind Nicholas. "You have been made clean."

"I am an unclean man. Yet, a joy has sprung inside my chest. I have much to learn and much to do—much to receive."

"That you do," Rigel said. "We must go on. Let us walk."

Rigel grasped Nicholas' hand and raised him to his feet. Rigel led the way. The stars burned above. The Milky Way and other galaxies whirled in the ether. Nicholas gazed upon the living heavens above him. He saw lights of many colors flitting between stars and galaxies and planets. The planets were luminous, large, and majestic. Mars gazed red; Nicholas felt braver. The moon, bright and silvery. Venus, blue, brimming with joy. Sol radiating and illuminating. Jupiter in its regal raiment whirled in the distance, Nicholas' heart yearned to meet the King of this world.

"Are we going to the King?" Nicholas asked.

"Yes, but we must walk through rough terrain first. Then we will reach the great city."

Suddenly, bright light shone before them as though the sun had risen immediately. Nicholas looked behind him. It was the same, dark solar—stars and planets in darkness. But before him was light. It was like a divided sky Nicholas remembered seeing in Montana. Behind was a thick dark cloud covering miles of sky, brooding over the mountain—rain and lightning. But before him was bright, blue sky.

The day was hot. Before them lay a hilly land, dry and rocky.

They traveled silently as the atmosphere grew hotter. Nicholas surprisingly wasn't sweating nor was he thirsty.

"This land seems familiar to me. It's like the wilderness heading toward Jerusalem, except wandering won't take forty years," Nicholas said.

Rigel nodded.

They travelled on for a very long time. Nicholas' energy was fading. His excitement of reaching a city waned and he shuffled on. His legs weary, his body ready to drop. "Rigel, may we stop. I feel like I'm carrying a millstone around my neck. I can't take another step further."

"Just up ahead. Once we reach the top of that hill, we only have a short distance to go from there," Rigel said.

They crested the dusty hill. The hill was white stone and the wind whirled dust in a cyclone. Nicholas heard someone shouting, but couldn't make out what was said. He saw a silhouette of what seemed to be a man in the distance.

"Who is that?" Nicholas said.

"Just a little further. It is someone whom you will cherish meeting," Rigel said.

They moved ahead. The shouting becoming clearer. "Further up and further in," the man said.

Finally they reached the man walking ahead of them, who was no longer shouting. The man wore a tweed jacket that was torn at the seams. It fit him rather comfortably, as though it was his favorite, most cherished coat. He wore a floppy hat upon his head and some disheveled trousers. Nicholas was reminded of one professor he had in university. The man seemed to fit the type. He ambled on as though taking a walking tour and Nicholas and Rigel happened to come alongside him.

"Ah, the atmosphere is too hot to be like Addison's, but I can go there another day," the man said. "And these dirty rags, I'd rather be dressed in clean linen again before coming before the King. But that has been arranged; I've been through the Jordan, through the refining fires. I'm just thinking aloud, sounding like a fool to this young gentleman. And how rude, I have not introduced myself. Clerk, N. W. Pleased to meet you."

Nicholas' heart leapt inside him, "Pleased to meet me? I'm more than pleased to meet you."

"Well it is humility in the ranks. Humility is thinking of oneself less after all. I have had my share of pride. I am made new, white as snow—where it is a pleasure to meet newcomers," Clerk said.

"Isn't it marvelous to see the skies alive as the ancients saw them? It is full of joy here. The atmosphere, heavens, everything is pregnant with substance—not vacuous and cold like back where I was before coming here," Nicholas said.

"This place is a marvel. I had hoped all my study of medieval constructs would have its culmination. Like all great art, we are directed to what the artist is saying, the poem itself, the painting itself, always pointing to 'the other.' But here all of art points to its Maker because here it is perfected. The poison of subjectivism, all the nonsense of the state of the artist's mind when he wrote, is finally engulfed in the light of pure truth. All that the great artists were plying pointed here. Ah, the wonder. Truth, beauty, goodness, all right here. But enough about that. Wisdom, peace, and that elusive joy is what you seek (which you will all find here, you have noticed glimpses). He sent me to encourage you in your journey, not talk about me. I understand there is much pain, a rift between you and your beloved," Clerk said.

"Yes, this is true. How. . . how did you know? The king of this land told you? I heard he knows all. My wife doesn't love me any longer it seems. Or we've gotten bored. The curse of decadence the ennui and acedia of our age that we suffer. Or she resents me for working all the time. I don't know, exactly," Nicholas said. "But I have wandered as well."

"To love at all is to be vulnerable. Love anything, and your heart will certainly be wrung and possibly broken. If you want to make sure of keeping it intact, you must give your heart to no one, not even to an animal. Wrap it carefully round with hobbies and little luxuries; avoid all entanglements; lock it up safe in the casket or coffin of your selfishness. But in that casket—safe, dark, motionless, airless—it will change. It will not be broken; it will become unbreakable, impenetrable, irredeemable. Do not harden your heart toward her. She may love you yet. Unless it is a selfish love not remembering the other, giving to the other as Christ loves His church," Clerk said.

"But why does loving another bring pain and such suffering?" Nicholas said. "I'd rather be about my business, reading, star-gazing, writing than have to deal with the tragedy love seems to move toward—an end."

"*To love at all is to be vulnerable. Love anything, and your heart will certainly be broken. If you want to make sure of keeping it intact, you must give your heart to no one. In that darkness it will become unbreakable. The only place where you can be perfectly safe from all the dangers and perturbations of love is Hell,*" Clerk said. "*Agape is the best of loves. It forgets itself. Yet it makes the receiver (you and her) more than yourself. Agape: when the true God arrives, only then do the half-gods remain. Without God who is divine love (agape), the half-gods become devils or vanish. And it is us, you and me, we are God's greatest achievement in creation—human beings made in His image and likeness—male and female. God's divine love is what moves us to love others.*"[1]

"'Batter my heart three-personed God. To break, blow, burn, and make me new.' So it is the King who transforms the heart from inwardness to becoming like Him, in loving others as Christ loves," Nicholas said.

"It is as Paul said marriage ought to be. It is the image of Christ and His church. Loving one another as He loves us—a broken, marred, wounded person. It is not one plus one equals two. It is one times one equals one with the mystery of individuality nonetheless. To love brings suffering, not because it is punishment, but because it cries out 'something is wrong here.' Christ makes us aware of our own shortcomings, our sin, and we can only fall at His feet and be restored—admitting our fallenness. Yet, like the

---

1. From C. S. Lewis' *Four Loves*.

King that He is, He welcomes His subjects back, 'rise and sin no more,'" continued Clerk.

"How do I love her again—there is nothing left to give or to receive. My selfishness has engulfed myself—my whole being. I have worn her down with insults as the rain erodes a hardened stone over decades. Until it cracks and is split in two," Nicholas said.

"You have confessed and must be restored. You are being restored as you journey on toward the city. You have been washed in water—leaving your dross behind as an oil slick. You are made clean, but there is fire and blood yet. As Elijah built the altar of twelve stones and the meat and blood were consumed in the fire on the mountain of Carmel, so your sin, pain, giving insult was burnt on the altar; you are being refined in this land—as small slivers fall from you: hatred, covetousness, self-pity, insult, slander, lust, sloth, acedia, fear, hatred, idolatry. These fall from you as you near the city. But your completion will not occur until fire and blood renew you in the room set aside for you."

"What do you mean by all of this?" Nicholas said.

"I will lead you to the city and to this room. You will understand when we arrive," Clerk said. "For now let us enjoy what is around us and what we will come upon in only moments."

As N.W. Clerk led Nicholas with Rigel just behind, they spoke of all the things upon the earth and what will become of all of creation. They spoke of fire and ice. Of the strength given to creatures of the King: one given joviality, another courage, another peace, another joy, another renewal, another wisdom, yet how all given by One who is in three—not separate spirits, but one, strengthening the people to call upon the King of this land.

Nicholas pondered all these things in his heart. Yet his mind could not grasp all that was taught to him. They crested another hill. Nearby, Nicholas heard singing. He looked in the direction the singing came from. Glancing left, he saw a light in a nearby cave and a man cooking something while singing a pleasing melody. The man said, "Come, sup with me. Come."

Nicholas walked toward the cave. N. W. Clerk walked beside him, but Rigel stayed upon the hill. Nicholas stooped down entering the cave.

"Are you coming?" Nicholas asked Clerk.

"No, I'll be here waiting for you." At that, Clerk pulled out a pipe from his jacket pocket and started puffing, the smoke made ringlets around him, floating toward the heavens.

"Come. Sit with me a while," the man said.

The fire he had was low, almost red and white coals. Small fish lay upon stones that lay near the hottest coals. "Here, eat some fish. I freely give what is given me."

Nicholas took a piece of the fish and ate. It was the best tasting fish he had ever had, but as soon as he swallowed it, he forgot what it had tasted like. All he knew was it satisfied.

The man wore a tattered robe that looked like burlap. He had gnarled hands, long clean hair. His face was neither young nor old—it was full of peace, wisdom behind his eyes. Strength exuded from this man. Nicholas felt he was before a powerful man, yet supping with the man felt like supping with a long-time friend.

"What brings you to the city?" the man asked.

"I didn't know there was a city, until Rigel (over on the hill) and N. W. Clerk led me toward it.

"Yet you are seeking something," the man said.

"Yes," Nicholas said.

"What you seek, you will find in the city. You will be welcomed, you will be transformed. You will be yourself, yet something more because the King wills it. He makes all who they are. And you are answering His call. You are being led to freedom, to peace, to joy, to life."

"How do you know this?" Nicholas said, his heart burning within him. "How could I know where I was going?"

"Yet you are willing to follow. Just because you are being led to the water with help does not make you weak. You have been taught to find on your own—to hack out the wilderness and make a place all by yourself. But it takes many to lead us to truth and to life. These are not happenstance—meeting Rigel, Clerk, me. Now, continue on toward the city. Many will meet you in the room you are being led to. You will not be the same. Now go."

At the command of the man, Nicholas ran out of the cave. Clerk was smoking and pondering the heavens. "He told me to go toward the city. We will meet many in the room there."

Clerk and Nicholas walked toward the hill Rigel was waiting upon gleaming in the light. Nicholas looked back toward the cave, but nothing—the firelight, the man—was there. They walked on, the planets following their courses in the heavens.

Chapter 5

There was a red hue in the sky. The three travelers walked on toward the direction of the city. Nicholas wasn't sure where this city was, but he was certain Rigel knew. They walked on in the heat of the day. The light of Sol spurring them on. The light of wisdom to guide their way.

The landscape was rocky. Some sparse vegetation grew on the rocky soil. There was mossy growth and lichen-like plants growing on the rock and the few scrub trees. In certain areas there was green moss-like growth that followed a curving line that went on to the edge of the horizon.

"Was there a river here at one point?" Nicholas said.

"There was. But it is the dry season now," Rigel said. "Though the water does not flow right now, the ground holds some of the water, which allows this green growth to grow in the arid climate."

Nicholas stepped into the green growth. His foot sunk slightly. It was comforting to his tired feet. He reached down and touched the green. It was soft to the touch and welcoming as a soft place to lie down after a long, weary day.

"May we rest here for a short time?" Nicholas said.

"We may. I forget that not all has been strengthened within you. The spirit is willing but the body grows weary. In time your body will have strength and perfection. The King will see to that. But for now, let us rest for a while," Rigel said.

N. W. Clerk sat in the green growth and looked into the heavens, contemplating the beauty above. Nicholas lay on his back and also pondered the beauty he saw above. The planets sailing in their orbits. Their beautiful colors: reds, oranges, fire-red and orange, blues, indigoes, dark azure, magnificent greens—aqua, chartreuse, topaz. And the blood reds, rubies and maroons. The colors were all a beautiful mixture in perfect beauty. A golden light was the backdrop of these numerous hues.

"Why is it we always seek wisdom and knowledge? Will we ever fully know?" Nicholas said.

"Wisdom is an ever present ongoing journey. We learn for the sake of learning. Not necessarily for use. The depths of wisdom are in all places. If we are looking. Wisdom. There is only One who is wisdom. When we seek Him, we will begin to know. The beginning of wisdom is the fear of God. Not a fear that paralyzes and makes us cower in oppression. But a fear that we have for One we greatly respect. We bow before Him in humility. For we are like dried wheat before him.

"Wisdom contains all. We only discover and see glimpses of understanding. But we are not mindless creatures. We have a likeness to the King. That is how we can recognize wisdom . . . the truth of matters . . . the goodness and the beauty of things It is the King of wisdom who teaches us to put these things in right order. Our loves are out of order. We are like wine. The older we get and the more we listen . . . to the King . . . to the whispering music of the spheres . . . the more we see, the more we understand," Clerk said.

"You speak riddles. But I understand in part. We must plant ourselves in the soil that will nurture us. I understand this. My life has been in such disarray, it has been difficult to discipline my mind and heart in these things of wisdom. I have been consumed by use. What can I do with what I have learned? Is all I think. What use can I acquire with knowledge and wisdom? What can I gain from these things? I have lost the understanding of wisdom's main purpose," Nicholas said.

"Don't allow delight and wonder to die. When I read the lines 'Balder the beautiful is dead, is dead,' a longing sprung in my heart. For the light of wisdom I sought had also died within me. I had been preoccupied in rationalizing my world: the consequence was that the light of wisdom died within me. I stuffed all the delight and wonder in the depths of myself. But it sprang forth again, child-like and beautiful. Love takes time to birth. Our main purpose in life is not use at all. Beauty has no use, except to please the eye. But beauty is necessary. Does not something stir within you when you recognize beauty? The beauty of colors. The beauty of shape and form. The beauty of a candle burning within a red sconce? A field of wheat bent in the wind. The stars and planets above. A vivid violet growing amidst gray concrete. An etching of the Sacred Heart of Jesus on a concrete wall in Auschwitz, Poland. And of course there are distortions of beauty, there is ugliness. But we know what those things are. But in beauty something within us lights up. Our countenance changes, transforms into the light of glory. In wisdom is our heart alight in delight and wonder. Pure rationalism is dead. But wisdom brings life. Seek the King and all these things will be given you. Let light guide and transform you. It is already happening in you," Clerk said.

Nicholas looked toward Rigel. Always standing, guarding, vigilant, alert, never weary. Nicholas lay back again and watched the beautiful dance of colors above him. He delighted in the light above and the conversation with Clerk. But the conversation had met its end. Nicholas basked in the silence, a contentment washing over him and a peace settling within him. He listened to the pregnant silence. And in it, he swore he heard some beautiful indescribable music in perfect harmony. He closed his eyes. The silence with a hint of melody in it made his mind wander into a restful sleep.

As Nicholas slept, he had a vision: He walked in the dark. He was following a sidewalk, the streetlamps giving him light and direction. But he walked in a panic, in a hurry, not sure where he was going or where he would end up. He reached a fountain. It was blurry at first, but then came into focus. The fountain was not running, it wasn't spilling its streams of water. He knelt at the fountain and noticed the stagnant black water within it, reflecting his image softly lit by an unknown source. His reflection was of an aged man, with black circles under his eyes. His skin haggard and wrinkled. He looked closer, squinting in horror at what he saw. He touched his face where it seemed there were scales on his right cheek. As he touched his face, he felt the scales, but the image and the scene abruptly changed as they do in dreams.

Nicholas now stood at the middle of a dark, empty room. There was echoing music playing like a distant memory. It was a haunting sound. He felt utterly alone and dismal. Afraid. In despair. There were balloons on the floor around him. A door opened in the distance. A bright light flooded into the room. Nicholas focused on the light the door allowed into the empty room. A woman, blurry at first, appeared at the door and started to walk toward him. Nicholas didn't know who she was. But as she came closer, Nicholas could see how beautiful she was. She looked angelic. Her face perfectly symmetrically beautiful. Her skin milky-white, smooth and perfect. Her hair strong and healthy, lustrous, beautiful. She wore a sleek black party dress. It cleaved to her perfect form. She smiled at Nicholas. Nicholas smiled back. She came closer. And as she did, her countenance changed. The light was squelched as she approached Nicholas. The beautiful woman's face was a breath away from Nicholas' face, but instead of smiling, she sneered at Nicholas. Her teeth perfectly aligned, the canines sharp and predatory. She whispered to Nicholas, "Come with me. I will give you all that you need and all that you desire." Her lips moist and welcoming, breath sweet as honey. She walked toward the door on the far end. Nicholas began to follow her. But someone else came into the room. It was N. W. Clerk. He saw the woman and told her "Stop."

She halted her footsteps. So did Nicholas. N. W. Clerk walked to where the beautiful woman stood. He then did the unexpected. He tore her dress off. In horror, she wilted to the floor. She was no longer beautiful. Her skin was ashen. Her legs were monstrous, with bony jagged teeth protruding. Her hair haggard, stringy, grey. Her mouth, no longer sweet but a maw gaping, open as in death.

The scene changed again. Nicholas walked with N. W. Clerk on the star-gazing plateau where he met Evenstar. The stars were bright and burning above. Orion prominent in the sky. Galaxies and nebulas swirling in the darkness.

"Thank you for saving me in the empty room," Nicholas said.

"I was only sent. It's easier to obey in this land than it was back home. Now, when I get the call, I move, not tarrying or procrastinating like I used to do. The spirit is willing and so is my body and my mind. Not trying to convince myself that someone else will take care of things or a thousand reasons not to heed the call," N. W. Clerk said.

"Theosis. Glory. Our wills, our hearts, our bodies, our whole being is taught to conform to the King's will. It's much more difficult at home, as you said. But here it seems easier. But my will still wishes to do what it wants. Will it change or be transformed—as I keep hearing from Evenstar and the man in the cave?" Nicholas said.

"Yes. Of course. All in time. This place is all in motion. Motion is life. Stillness, death. Our movement, our motion is powered by love. The One who loves sets in motion the entire cosmos. The stars and the galaxies and the nebulas; our hearts, minds, our wills. They are all set in motion by the love of the One who loves us perfectly. That motion transforms our wills to love others. Here we hear it more clearly and are ready to obey more swiftly. Set to motion more willingly," Clerk said.

"Is this the music I started hearing before falling into this dream?" Nicholas said.

"Precisely. The music of the spheres. Love, its origin," Clerk said.

Nicholas awoke. He smiled at the sight before him. N. W. Clerk stood over him smiling. Clerk reached out his hand. Nicholas did the same.

"I've got you, brother," Clerk said. Clerk helped Nicholas to his feet.

Chapter 6

The daylight never ceased. The warm air and the light enveloped the landscape in tranquility. Though in the wilderness, Nicholas didn't feel like he was lost or would never reach his destination. The vision he had had never left his psyche. The feelings and the besetting sin of always seeking someone else, something else haunted him. It was lead in his heart, in the pit of his stomach. Nicholas always sought someone else to save him. As his marriage soured, though his romanticism overwhelmed him into choking silences, he would admire beautiful women who would enter his book shop. Their gossamer features. Their expert clothing; some professionals, others artists. He admired both. But he dared never speak to them, except the usual book talk or sales points. He admired their mystery. Some hidden within themselves, Nicholas longing to draw them out. The shy beauty who had deep, still waters deep within. Books their only common subject. The book acting as the object to get a glimmer of the mystery of her being. The artist with their skilled matching eclectic and pleasing clothes. What they wore was art. The colors. The matching hues that Nicholas had to understand by looking at the color palette came to an artist naturally.

Then there were the confident professionals who knew who they were. Their expert clothing. Their fine matching luxurious jewels. Again, books and that longing for their confidence to rub off on Nicholas. Nicholas' temptations, the sirens, he created himself, within his own psyche . . . longing for the thing he could not have . . . the pear in the tree . . . to take would be a violation and wound to his intellect. His loves were out of order.

But there was one whom he admired and sensed admired him. At first she came to buy books. They had similar tastes. Nicholas recommending title after title. Then she started coming more often. And finally left notes at the cash register that he would find later. Nicholas was attracted to her, of course. But he was paralyzed in acting on any possible desire he had for her. As he walked in the heat of the day, he recalled her to his memory. Her green eyes. Her soft hands. Her styled, short hair with hints of blonde. Her sweet smile. Nicholas smiled to himself, lost in his thoughts. But he shook away his idle thinking, ready to speak to Clerk or Rigel to bring his idle wanderings to focus again.

But so lost in his thoughts, something had changed. Rigel and Clerk were nowhere to be seen. Nicholas continued to walk, not frightened that he had lost his companions at this point. The way became more rocky. Nicholas stumbled under foot. He almost fell several times. He stumbled over white rocks and stubbed his toes on many of them. The walk became more labored. He was walking uphill. "I figure I will be able to spot Clerk and Rigel at the top of this hill," Nicholas thought to himself.

He reached the top of the high place with bloodied knees and hands. He stopped walking, realizing he had reached the edge of a cliff. The valley far below him was nothing but brown landscape for miles and miles. He looked over the edge of the cliff, but became dizzy and stepped back. He was much higher than he ever realized. The walk up the hill wasn't that strenuous. "Where have I ended up now?" Nicholas said aloud.

"You are on the same precipice the King's son was on after wandering the desert, the wilderness for forty days. This is a high place where either true worship takes place or idol devotion occurs," said a voice behind him.

Nicholas turned toward the voice. He saw no one standing there. "Who are you?" he shouted. He looked left and right. Finally, at the corner of his eye, he saw a variation in his vision. He saw a wave in the air, much like one sees on a hot day, the heat shimmering from the asphalt. He focused on this variation. It became clearer. It now was a shimmering white glimmer, the length of six feet. It looked like a blade made of light.

"You see me now, do you not, mortal one?" it said.

"I do. Yes. What or who are you?" Nicholas said.

"I am but a servant. Like many whom you have met. I am here to reveal how things are. Who you are. What you were. Who you will be," the light said.

"What does that mean? Isn't that the age old question? Who am I? Haunting this post-modern world. The existential question," Nicholas said.

"Yes. But I only speak what I hear. And I have heard much about you. You are a wretched man. A wretched, lonesome man who cannot see where he is going," the light said.

"Yes. But I have already spoken to Evenstar. The coal has touched my lips. But I still sense the weariness of my fallenness. I know I am wretched, what I am. But no, I barely know *who* I am," Nicholas said.

"I am not finished. You also have a heart for your fellow sufferer. You understand suffering in a way that will comfort others who suffer. Yet, you have a thorn in your heart. Its name, acedia and the other lust. Lust for the things you cannot have. It is like a cloak that comforts you in your idleness and wandering of mind. Your love for beauty scorns your heart to turn a beloved into an It. A thing, an object. To do what you wish not to do but do nonetheless. Ethics and morality duel. Temptation—the Bower of Bliss—turns beauty into lust of the eyes; lust of the fallen flesh. Your countenance darkened. You pray in the secret parts of your heart for modesty and chastity to wrap your countenance in virtue and goodness. You even stare at an icon you do not understand to allow light into your whole being. The mind, the person in a duel with self. Then obsession takes you like a whirlwind, a tempest in your mind and in your heart. Circles and wheels about you. Emotions toiling wanton feelings desiring to act in affection that become affliction and passion for forbidden fruit, like the pear tree that Augustine goes on about. Thirsting and hungering for what is not yours. Dreaming to take the pear from the tree. The thou which you desire haunts your thoughts. The thoughts you have neglected for so long. Thou commands you to open the book commanding you otherwise: take and eat the bread and drink the wine. Which is thine given to thou. The fire of passion a consuming fire. But Thou a consuming eternal fire. Thou's perfected love calling for you to reside in him. But your countenance darkens, isolating your thoughts. A cage and chains that bind you from seeing. Seeing that the beauty you have always sought is the King. You long to see the world as it is. It is grief-stricken, dark, mysterious, lonesome, harsh, an anguish, but also a glory and a beauty. It is love that you lack. Not the fleeting and fickle eros or philia, but agape, the divine love that moves all. In love we see. We see the created order as in chains, but also as it was on the dawn of creation, the first day. Now you have seen a glimpse of the Last Day. When all things are as they should be. Perfect justice enacted. Perfect love permeating all things.

"You *are* a wretch, but you are also made worthy by the King's love. *Maranatha. Alleluia!*"

Nicholas' head full. His heart overflowing. His entire being overwhelmed with shame and joy. Nicholas fainted.

Chapter 7

The moon sailed across the sky with Venus in her silver wake. Love and beauty written in the sky. The two celestial bodies silver and blue, one setting the boundary, the other springing life. Venus setting the fertile ground, incense burning in the air, while Luna spells the boundary: chastity, and waters the fertile ground.

Nicholas awoke. It was dark. He only saw the moon and Venus in the night sky. The ground was wet beneath him, dew he supposed. The light being was absent. Nicholas was alone. But he did not feel alone or lonesome. But he didn't know how he would find his guide or friend again. Though it was dark, there was enough light from the moon to see by. Beside him was a bush, much like a holly bush with red berries, but the leaves were different. They were soft rather than spikes, but the same deep forest green. He reached out to grasp the berries. But at his touch, the bush burst into flame. Nicholas pulled his hand away swiftly. But there was no searing heat from the flames. The flames swirled, blue, orange, yellow consuming the bush, yet not turning it to ash or charcoal. The bush was consumed by flame, but not consumed. Nicholas was nearly dazzled by it. He looked deep into the heart of the burning bush. He could still see the red berries and the deep forest green leaves.

Within the flames he saw a face. At first, it was a pale, silver that transformed into a teal and then cobalt which again changed into an illuminated face of a woman. The woman also had a blue veil or head scarf. Her eyes deep and soft that exuded love. Her face changed into a dazzling white that nearly blinded Nicholas. Nicholas gasped and looked away briefly then back to the bush.

The image changed. He saw a man with similar features of the woman's. His face was stern, yet at peace. Nicholas could see his shoulders which were covered in what looked like a robe. His left shoulder was covered by blue cloth and the right covered by red. He also held a book that was open and his hand was raised in some type of blessing. He said nothing, but somehow by only seeing this man, Nicholas was undone. Nicholas looked deeply into the man's eyes and knew this man had the greatest love for him, for all creatures. Nicholas' face was dappled with tears, turning into rivulets upon his cheeks.

The image changed again. There was a stone table. Objects were being placed on the table one by one. Some of the objects were gold chalices. Others were an array of grains, all kinds of harvested foods and flowers. Still other objects were treasure and crafted things: like art, musical instruments, all manner of crafted items, many practical, many beautiful. Finally, an array of objects were placed on the stone table. One was an ivory statuette of a woman, breasts full, face in perfect form. The statuette was placed in the middle of the stone table. It was smashed upon the table. Another statuette was placed on the stone table. It was of a man with raised hands holding gold and silver in accolade. This, too, was smashed. There were more and more statuettes placed before the table that were smashed. Finally an effigy of a man sitting and contemplating drawn into himself was placed upon the stone table. Nicholas' heart ached, for contemplation was his most cherished. But he knew contemplation, as an introvert, could be used as an excuse to avoid people whom Nicholas loved and who loved him. This image, too, was smashed.

A voice said, "These things, these idols you have placed above the One true are taken from you now. But all things that are unshakable will remain. All things placed before the stone table are given back to the One true to be redeemed. They will be made new. Even though your idols have been destroyed, the good and pure aspects will be given back to you redeemed. Contemplation is good. Contemplation strengthens the inner man when planted in the soil of the King."

The image changed again. Swirls of colors. Reds and gold, greens and blues, bleeding into oranges and yellows. It was a mosaic. An autumnal festival of color. No artist could have captured all the shades and light of this burning bush. Then a voice came from the bush, "Follow the evening star and moon, they will lead you to the great city. Love and life and joy await you there. Go. Follow."

Nicholas jumped to his feet and ambled down the hill. A second wind bolstered his sail. He was ready to travel with his celestial guides. As he looked up at the moon and planet, he saw a bird fly in the moonlight. It cawed and by the sound of it, Nicholas recognized it as a hawk. The bird also flew in the direction of the celestial guides. Nicholas smiled. This adventure encompassed all the longing and imaginations he had held within him since childhood. Nicholas had always cherished hawks, spotting them in the woods, along with owls.

The silence in the night sky and the bright face of the moon and the flickering light of Venus while the hawk flew between earth and sky was music to Nicholas' entire being. He felt a joy rise within him. A sense of purpose. A sense of mending the brokenness within him.

How long had he yearned for such joy? It seemed all his life. Nicholas had forgotten what it was to feel content. His envy, depression, acedia had worn him down. Before entering this land, he was a shell of a man. Despairing, desiring someone else, desiring things he knew would never satisfy. But he lied to himself that anything would fill and mend his broken heart. Rationally, he knew nothing could quench his thirst or his appetite. His appetite was insatiable. Only one thing would ever satiate. He had already seen glimpses and met those who pointed him toward the true source of his desire. But in the thick fog of confusion, in the fallen chasms of this planet earth, irrationality reigned. In that world Nicholas was enslaved. But in this world he was liberated, set free from the enslavement of the demonic. The demonic: the irrational. The eyes of death. Seeing only death and never life. This was the trap Nicholas was a slave to, he now realized. His life was in the stinking grave, his mouth agape only knowing death. But this land was his glimpse into all as it ever should have been. Death did not reside here. All had been resurrected. All had life pulsing through its veins. Even the dry places, the wilderness breathed life and joy. What land was this? Had he truly entered the culmination of time, where there was no more time? But it was so familiar and similar, minus the malaise that plagued every being and the atmosphere of planet earth, where Nicholas had come from. Was this the earth at the culmination? Or was this an entirely different world? Another universe even. Or another dimension? But the moon, and Venus. And all the other planets of the solar system. It is the same world, but vastly different. It had the beauty of where Nicholas had come from, but without the death and destruction. The vegetation was lush and green and vibrant, even in the desert. He would find out the answers to his questions and where he was at the great city. He wondered if he would reach the city at first light. In his contemplation, he heard the faint whisper of melody and harmony in the atmosphere.

Chapter 8

Darkness immediately turned into first light. Sol lit the sky with quickened gold seemingly sent by Mercury. It was quit the spectacle. Instead of the sun rising slowly in the east, with orange and red tones, the day was illuminated immediately by Sol. It was night and then it was day; the first day.

Nicholas saw buildings spread all over a hill in the distance. They shimmered as though a mirage in desert heat. The light dancing off of distant towers of white stone. Squat rectangular buildings surrounded a central part of the city. In the center was a magnificent building, almost a cathedral castle stabbing toward the heavens. It shone in the light—a golden hue. It was magnificent and beautiful. The moon hung directly above the great castle and Jupiter, Mars, and Venus hovered nearby, their light brightly shining: dark red, red, and blue. This must have been the city Nicholas was looking for.

The hawk turned out to be an excellent guide. He still flew above and ahead of Nicholas, wings gliding, barely flapping to gain speed. The hawk rode upon wind as though a sailing vessel gliding upon still waters. The faithful hawk let out its screech. This caused Nicholas to look upon the horizon. He saw the city, of course, but also two slight figures, wavering silhouettes of people. "Could it be Rigel and Clerk?" Nicholas wondered.

Nicholas quickened his step. But the hawk was gone. His guide was no longer needed. He thanked the hawk silently. The way before him was smooth except for slight hills, like waves before him. A new breath and swiftness, an invigoration was upon him. Lightness of step; joy in his heart, new life, a warmth, a strength, a fragrance imbued his countenance. He crested the hills of the terrain before him with ease and with joy. Gone was his usual malaise and self-abnegation.

Nicholas finally caught up to his companions. The shapes that were slight and distant before were now close. And he confirmed they were Rigel and Clerk. There was no guilt or anger that he had toward them, which was strange. Because had he been home, if a friend abandoned him, only anger and guilt, figuring his friend didn't like him would envelope his psyche. Abandonment and rejection permeated his whole self in that other world, which seemed like a dream now. Maybe this was truly home and not his life at the bookstore and his failing marriage. But this was escapism, he knew. A Platonist to the core. But he couldn't analyze any longer.

"I'm glad I found you. I didn't think I'd see either of you again," Nicholas said. "Why didn't you wait for me? Well . . . I take that back. This is a strange land. At one moment, you are wandering the desert and another you are atop a high place . . . to mountainous heights."

"Yes. This place can be a mystery, but it is always in the hands of Providence. As we walked with you before in the lush green bed of the river, we were whisked away. Rigel said he was told to speed us along, ahead of you, though we lost you. It seems you needed to be alone for that time. I'm sure it was with purpose and meaning," Clerk said.

"It was with purpose. I saw something I had only read about once. A burning bush with brilliant hues no artist could ever capture. It was beautiful. And a voice spoke." Nicholas proceeded to share all he saw and heard. "The light spoke of my wretchedness and my quality. I was overwhelmed. I'm not sure why he reminded me of my wretchedness."

They kept walking. Clerk was silent, but then spoke. "It is because you are not fully remade or fully perfected and transformed. There is still dross from the silver being refined still floating atop the molten metal. I am not fully remade either. I still wear rags. When we come before the King, we will be redressed—as white as snow. But the hope is we are being remade. The work has not been completed yet. But it will. Patience is the enemy of the hasty. But again, be encouraged, in the illuminated bush, you saw the face of the King and the face of his revered mother. This is a high honor to be chosen to see them *before* seeing them. You will meet them in the great castle at the center of the city. We were whisked away for a reason. That you would encounter these events. Rigel told me we would set the trail before you and he would go back and find you."

"Now I understand," Nicholas said. "The hawk. You were also the hawk." Nicholas said this to Rigel and smiled.

Rigel also smiled.

"This land is a mystery. But I like it," Nicholas said.

They continued to walk toward the city, which was becoming nearer and nearer. Further up and further in they went.

The three travelers reached the outer wall of the city. The wall wasn't very high and would offer no protection from invaders. But there were large gates with banners at their tops. The gates had no doors or blockades. But the ways were barred by a single guardian. A sole man stood there. He smiled.

"You must be here for the feast," he said.

"What feast?" Nicholas said.

"Do not cause yourself anxiety. The King told me you were coming. Welcome to the great city. Step through the gate, enjoy all that you see. You will meet many. Some you have known, some you know of, others you never knew. For on the day when all awaken, for your world is asleep, there will be a great feast. A time of rejoicing. You see this time in your own place—where you came from— but you see through the eyes of death. So you see with rejoicing *and* mourning. But there will be a day when the Last Day will be present. It will be much like what you have seen and encountered here in this land. But I must be silent, for I am delaying your journey. Go ahead. Look for the home with the red banner waving in the wind. That is where you must go."

Nicholas, N. W. Clerk, and Rigel walked through the gate. Within the city walls, there was a calm, even though it bustled with people. People from all places of the world. There was peace. Not a disassociation and niceness, but the weight of kindness and a peace where there is no toil or strife. All know who they are and what they are supposed to be, greeting each other with joy and love.

As the three walked through the streets, there was a joy that Nicholas could only compare to Christmastime. A genuine care and joy and life within people as they greeted one another or giving donations to Salvation Army or buying hot chocolate for those outside in the cold. Or that anticipation of the birth of the Savior. There was an anticipation in the people in the streets of this city. A people under a good ruler. A people who knew what they were supposed to do. A people in love. Joy, wonder, and delight in their eyes. Some hummed as they walked. Others sang joyful songs. But it wasn't embarrassing as it might be for Nicholas back in his hometown. He heard some proclaim *Exultate* or *In te, Domine, speravi* or *Jubilate Deo*. These words, Nicholas had heard when he had been going to church or saw them in the psalter. Most of the time, these words had been said through dry throats, parched lips. Not with joy as these people were saying. These people were embodiments of these praises. "This is what it is like to walk in joy," Nicholas thought to himself, as his eyes were tearing. Joy, elusive in his other life. Where he was from, he would scorn and envy people who lived in joy, or seemed to live in such joy. After all, Nicholas was a modern, always a skeptic. But here, he nearly wept for the joy that these people exuded. He too longed for that joy.

"It's beautiful, isn't it?" N. W. Clerk interrupted Nicholas' train of thought.

"It truly is," Nicholas said.

"It is beauty and joy that we seek. It is the delight and wonder that a child has that we must hold onto. It is simple to do here. But I remember it being so difficult back in your state of life, Nicholas," N. W. Clerk said.

"We always wish we could keep that moment of joy, a moment of when we were happy. That thing we longed for though we couldn't necessarily name it. Like the blue flower or the Island in the West. But joy is here. It was never a thing, was it, Clerk?"

"No. It never was a thing. It is a person. That person who is life itself; joy itself. The one who gives us these things when we give it back to him to be redeemed. When we give our joys to him, then it is only redeemed and made as it truly is. When we give ourselves, not parts of ourselves, but our whole self, then it is when we are transformed into His likeness. We were broken. But he remakes us. The image never lost, but fully restored by him," Clerk said.

"These are great mysteries and depths beyond me. It reminds me of the seed. It is such a small thing. But it contains all the nutrients it needs to become a tree. Like the acorn. It is so small. But grows into a magnificent tree. A strong tree. It seems the seed dies, buried in the ground, but blossoms from the dust, from seeming death into something more glorious than where it started. This is a beautiful mystery. We are teeming with life, especially when we know where to go for the fertile soil and water. Amazing what dormant ideas in my mind come back to life in this place," Nicholas said.

"The man in the cave must have told you something. And it seems to be happening," Clerk said.

"Yes. He told me more dross would be left behind and transformation would take place," Nicholas said.

As they walked, they passed several buildings where people were delightfully putting mosaics on the stucco or painting beautiful multi-colored murals or beautiful blue azure, gold, and yellow murals. The art was breathtaking. There were pastoral images, beautiful golden sunrises, beautiful flowers and trees blooming, the full range of marine life or beastiary. All of creation was painted, sculpted, made into mosaic all over the city.

Finally, they saw up ahead a two story building with a red banner waving in the wind.

"This is the place," Rigel said. "Follow me."

Chapter 9

They entered the building. The interior walls were painted, again, in the mosaic themes that Nicholas saw in the city. An ocean blue covered the walls with scenes of animals in arrays of colors. Some mosaics were tile and others painted. The downstairs was an open room. Clean and sparse. The three moved toward the back of the room. There was a staircase. They ascended. At the top of the stairs was another open room. The walls were painted gold, red, and blue. There was a regal quality about the room. But there was no throne to be seen. The room was lit by the natural illumination of Sol. There were no shadows in this room. Nothing could hide. But there was nothing to hide from or cower before. This room had only welcome about it. The tone of the room was salutation, reception, hailing all who entered with open arms and warmth.

The room was very large and filled with people. There was a low table at the center and many surrounded the table sitting on floor cushions. The others, who filled the entire room, were either standing or sitting on the floor or leaning against the wall. Some sat in the many deep windowsills. Joy radiated from each person's face. They were aglow.

There was some chatter in the room. But not from a cacophony of conversation. All the people were looking toward someone in communion. All attentive toward one. Nicholas gazed toward the person all were transfixed upon. At the low table, sat a man.

The man, Nicholas recalled, was like the man he saw within the burning bush, but also reminiscent of the man in the cave. His eyes deep, exuding wisdom, peace and strength. The man looked toward Nicholas.

"Come here timid one," the man said to Nicholas.

Nicholas looked left and right uncertain to whom this man was speaking to.

"Yes, Nicholas, I mean you. Come here. Sit beside me," the man said.

Nicholas stepped forward with a gentle push from Clerk. He passed through the crowd with people smiling and shaking his hand and pats of friendship upon his back. The welcome was not overwhelming, though Nicholas was not fond of crowds. It was a communion of people who knew and showed genuine and pure friendship, love, and approval. Nicholas came beside the man who summoned him, but only stood there forgetting what to do.

"Sit, my friend," the man said and laughed heartily. The laugh was jovial and true. It rang of mirth like that of Father Christmas with the power of a great waterfall or thunder, but without the danger. "I am of the order of Melchisedec. My king is Jupiter, its meaning. The red, the jovial. The wounded ruler who fills all things, exacting perfect justice, perfect mercy, perfect love."

Nicholas sat. He noticed that Melchisedec, Nicholas decided to call him, for all he heard was that name, not "order of," had on a thick robe, one side red and the other blue. "I saw you in the vision, the burning bush."

"That you did." He laughed again. "What was told to you was difficult to remember. Was it not? But the King is always merciful to those who turn their ways. All this time you have followed the river, which led you to the pool. Baptized in its waters, you were given strength and renewal that strengthened you on your journey. Then you ascended the mountain to the plateau, where you confessed, laying your fault before Evenstar. Then you followed the green riverbed. Where visions were given you. Then you got lost, as the mortal body will do. And you were again reminded of your fault. But also encouraged. Now you are here. We were all waiting for you. Now that you are here, we can begin."

The room filled with a tremendous pressure. The golden light that came through the many windows changed from gold to red. A rushing sound filled the room. And what seemed like flickering flames alighted upon each person's head.

Melchisedec said, "Receive the spirit of truth. He will teach you everything and remind you of all that I have said. You have opened the book and have read. Truth will illuminate these words and make them come to life within you. Take and eat. For Melchisedec lives by bread and wine alone. Also receive the bread and wine I give all of you. Peace I leave with you; my peace I give to you."

At that the rushing sound ceased and the red hue subsided. There was gold light coming through the windows again. Melchisedec held a loaf of bread and broke it. He tore a piece and gave it to Nicholas. Nicholas ate it. Then Melchisedec took a cup of wine and let Nicholas partake. "Cherish this in your heart. You know what this means. Your heart and mind remember. Life springs inside of you. Abide in me and I will abide in you. You have been cleansed by the word I have spoken to you. I am the vine; you the branches. Apart from me you can do nothing."

Nicholas' whole person was filled with a joy he had never felt before. He had no words. But all he could do was embrace the man beside him—Melchisedec. Nicholas' face reddened, but a mirthful laugh bellowed from Melchisedec's belly. "Now go, embrace life, take in joy. Though the burden of time and its heartache bear on your shoulders, remember joy. Remember this moment. Remembrance will take you back to this point, just as we were taken back to that blessed moment in the Upper Room at the Last Supper. But now each day is filled with the presence of the King because it is the new day . . . every day. Filled with joy and peace, life and love. The fog of your world will dim what you have seen and known here. When you return, you will remember less and less. But the Spirit will aid you in remembering, for he is the Spirit of truth and of all memory. Always illuminating. Always reminding. Your pain will turn into joy. Now go. You must meet the king with your companions. He will be pleased to see you again. Now go. Be filled with delight and wonder again." At this Melchisedec touched Nicholas' forehead. A warmth emanated from Melchisedec's hand and permeated Nicholas' forehead.

"It is a true joy to know you and to meet you. Must I leave this place?" Nicholas said.

"You must. We must always move on to where we are called. But I will be with you until the end of the age. Now go. We will meet again," Melchisedec said.

Nicholas rose to his feet. As he left, he embraced those who surrounded him and those who were in his path toward the staircase where Rigel and Clerk awaited him.

They left the Upper Room stepping down the stairs to the first floor. At the bottom of the staircase, Nicholas touched the banister. Something strange and amazing happened. At his touch, the banister was covered in holly leaves with bright red berries. They weren't miraculously cut from a holly tree and transported there, they grew there.

"That was weird," Nicholas said.

"Don't you mean miraculous?" Clerk said. "Mirth and life are springing from your fingertips. It is like the river being unchained from the bridge. Or the dull classroom sprung to life with life-giving words. Or the dance of fauns in the moonlight with blazing fire. And the dryads emblazoning flowers on the spring trees after a barren winter."

"Yes. Very much so. But it is still surprising, to say the least," Nicholas said.

"Of course. All things surprising are this way. But it is joy. And wonder. And delight. That wonderful childlike wonder," Clerk said.

They walked together out of the building and started walking toward the center of the city. The tall tower of the castle their guidepost.

Chapter 10

Jollity cleaved to Nicholas as he and his friends walked toward the center of the city. The streets were alive with many souls. Some were creating images upon the walls of buildings and homes, making the journey a wonder and a beauty to look upon. Others were conversing. Nicholas especially looked at each person's face. Joy radiated from them. Their countenance was light, there was no trace of shadow or melancholy. The three companions continued their walk. Up ahead it looked as though there was a dead end. But as they came closer, it was a wall that blocked the way forward, but there were alleys to the left and to the right.

The wall was white. There was nothing peculiar about it except that there were no colors or paint on the wall. It was beautiful in its pure white stone. A blank canvas. But Nicholas imagined something in his mind that would enhance the wall. For no particular reason, Nicholas touched the wall. It was cold. Nicholas swept his hand across the wall. Smooth in some places and rough in others, like many stones. When he removed his hand, where he had swept his hand there was a cobalt color that came out.

Rigel said, "Keep your hand on the wall."

Nicholas did. He put his palm flat on the wall. Something incredible happened. The wall was being painted. The cobalt hue served as the background and a green hue infused itself into the blue. The image continued to form. A valley with a blue backdrop and a tree near an azure river. The moon rested in the sky with a red Mars in martiality and a lighter shade of blue for Venus. While Jupiter was forming with its red, oranges, creams blending together in swirls. Saturn in a greenish-blue with its rings—looking like ice reminding of mortality. Bright Mercury near Sol, yellow and gold respectively. Then three figures formed on the image—representing the three travelers. Nicholas removed his hand. His hand print blended into the painting. If you looked at the image from the right angle, you could see Nicholas' prints. It was his signature, he thought.

"It is wonderful to use our imagination without hindrance of our ego. Art will always be. It is a mirror from the one who created all things. All that was made is art. Art reflects the good, the true and the beautiful. We were surrounded by ugly art in our age, or art that was claimed as good art, but its distinctive did not convey truth, beauty or goodness. It only reflected death, nihilism, and consumption. But there is always good art. You just have to know how to see it. Art is love of light. And we know who the maker of light is, do we not?" N. W. Clerk said.

"Yes. Art as it is meant to be does capture the light of wisdom and truth and beauty and goodness. I remember the nihilistic forms passing as art which only reflected the maker's view of a meaningless world which he happened to inhabit. Art should raise our beings upward, not downward. We know where we end up, as dust. But it is the one longing for reunion with our Maker who desires to rise. To rise out of chains that hold us down. This is not escapist talk. But we long for the matter and form that we shape with our imagination to be the perfected form. Form *matters*. Even the shades in Hades had form, only not a solid form . . . the same in the Divine Comedy. In Paradise the forms are united again in perfection. The body with the mind and spirit. This is the longing that good art portrays. It longs for this perfection and for the perfect One. If only I could destroy the shackles that hinder my mind from thinking of the perfect One, in participating with body, spirit, and mind to move in love toward the ground of my being . . . the King is the one whom I have sought all along. Isn't he?"

"You are beginning to see. Transformation, what delight. Meeting with the one of Melchisedec has helped you see more clearly," N. W. Clerk said.

"He has. But where can we go that will drain the guilt and fault that resides in my mind. The thoughts and deeds that haunt me and stay with me in this mortal body. It is being remade, yes. This I see, but I still feel its sluggishness," Nicholas said.

"Come. We will meet a woman of high esteem who will help you forget all that has weighed you down. Not to forget out of escape. But forgetting by the act of forgiveness," Rigel said.

Rigel led the way. The three went left leaving the new image Nicholas had created. The alleyway winded through the city. It was a meandering path through a wall of shops and homes. It was reminiscent of the alleys in Jerusalem or in Egypt. All the while, they ascended. The three meandered through shops where indigo cloth and sandals and wares were sold or given away, Nicholas could not tell. The purple cloth set on poles serving as a ceiling closed in the bazaar. Farther down the path there were white walls on either side. Only the golden blue sky could be seen above and the castle toward the right. The walls and the buildings on left and right blocked the view of the rest of the city. It was like traveling through a chasm, rock on either side, uncertain where the quick left turns and right turns would end up.

Finally, they were through the meandering path. Before them was the town square. A fountain stood in the center. There were nine paths concentrically from the midpoint—the fountain. A path straight ahead led directly to the castle on a hill. Likenesses of lions surrounded the fountain. Clear waters shooting toward the heavens above. The water reflecting golden hues. The spray forming rainbows and seeming like sparks flying from forged metal. Four pillars were at each corner of the fountain, but three more pillars stood amongst the other four. Nicholas saw a total of seven pillars.

The motion of the water, the pillars, and the granite lions drew the eye upward. In the sky above, Nicholas could see three planets converging. Rigel led Nicholas and Clerk toward one of the pillars where a woman stood. She smiled and spoke to Rigel. Nicholas could not hear what was said, the sound of the waters muffled his hearing. The woman wore a red shawl that covered her head. In fact, the cloth covered her whole body. There was blue cloth peaking from her neck. Her skin tan. She was beautiful.

She beckoned Nicholas forward, summoning him with her hand. She smiled. She looked intently into Nicholas' eyes. Her eyes piercing. Nicholas saw galaxies in her irises. She held depths of wisdom and a love that women in love only knew. She pressed her hand to Nicholas' face, and her tender smile and tender eyes swept over Nicholas. Her hand was very warm.

She said, "You have been in much pain. You have allowed love and fire of love to only burn a miniscule flame. Your heart has been broken. You weep in the night. But you hide yourself in the day. Not letting anyone in, not friends, not even your wife. Your heart has grown cold and hard, like a pressed coal in the heart of the earth. In the darkest and coldest cavern. But there is hope. For under such pressure, the coal becomes a diamond to be dug out of the heart of the earth. A dazzling stone, refracting all the colors of the cosmos. Your heart is also a seed that has died. It has been buried. But the waters have cared for this seed. Your faults and sins have weighed you down. Your countenance darkened by these things. Your idle imaginings haunt you. You want beauty to save you. But you know beauty alone cannot do this, though you long for it to save you. The sirens of your psyche have been exposed. The selfishness and blindness brought to light. But you are beginning to see three lead you toward Truth, Beauty, and Goodness. They have filled you with hope and life and joy. Be still now. Let me draw water from the fountain of Lethe. That you may forget the darkness of your own heart. The secret longings within you that draw you away from Reality, from the Good."

She withdrew her hand from Nicholas' face. She knelt and picked up a clay jug from the ground, dipped it into the fountain water behind her and filled the jug. She withdrew the jug and put it to Nicholas' lips.

"Now drink. Sins will be forgotten, but your whole being will be filled with love which sustains and moves the spheres, moves all things," she said.

Nicholas drank the water. It was cool, but went down his throat with warmth. It had an earthen taste, like leaves and rich soil. As he drank, thoughts of running away, from escaping into his books, an adulterous heart, running away with a beautiful woman, forgetting his wife, neglecting his friends, neglecting the poor all flooded to the forefront of his psyche. When he finished drinking from the jug, all these images vanished. He could not recall any sin or wrongful thing he had done or left undone. A great burden was lifted from him. And in this, he somehow felt lighter. As though a true weight had dropped off of him.

The woman smiled. "In Magdala, I met a man who knew all I had done. I was filled with lust and an appetite for wrongful things. But this man touched my face and showed me what true love was. To lay down his life for the whole world. To forgive. He told me to go and sin no more. I followed him from that day forth. I even saw him die a horrible death. But I was the first to witness his grave empty." Her eyes filled with tears. "But I remember in joy, not sorrow. My eyes are wet with joy. Now go and sin no more. Be filled as I was filled with love that changes hearts and ways of living. You are going to the King. He will show you the way home. But we will meet again." She embraced Nicholas and gave him a small vial placed in his hand.

"What's this?"

"Spikenard. I washed his feet with this very fragrant oil." She smiled with a joy that lit her face.

Chapter 11

The three friends went on from there to meet the King. They walked several meters, then descended granite stairs with gold flecks within the stone. They crossed a small valley where toppled marble pillars and granite stones similar to gravestones lay in ruin. They were crumbling and forming a valley of silt with broken teeth jutting out. Eventually, Nicholas imagined, it would be a smooth way and the eroded stones would serve as soil where wild flowers would grow in a multitude of colors.

Before them was a staircase that ascended a small mountain the height of about nine hundred feet. They ascended. Clerk talked about poetry and the psalms. Rigel sang one of the psalms of ascent. The psalms the Hebrews would sing as they ascended the hill and the Temple stairs.

"I lift up my eyes to the hills—from where will my help come?" Rigel sang.

"He is your keeper; he is your shade at your right hand. He will keep your life," Clerk said as Rigel sang.

Then the melody changed. "For there the thrones of judgment were set up, the thrones of the house of David. Peace be within your walls, and security within your towers. For the sake of the house of the Lord our God, I will seek your good. To you I lift up my eyes, O you who are enthroned in the heavens!" Rigel sang with a melodious tone. It was as though it was sung on the first day of all things, creating harmony and order that could never be shaken. As Rigel sang, three ladies ran past the three travelers. They were young, less than middle age, but not adolescents. Their joy reminded Nicholas of children, of innocence, but at a glimpse of one of the lady's eyes, Nicholas saw timelessness. These women were joyous as though in youth, but aged as a sage, wisdom in their eyes. Their gossamer dresses sailed past. Their forms ascending with speed and delight.

"The three virtues arise. Their joy remains with us though they pass us. They go before all things. Faith, Hope and Love have guided us unseen through these lands. Their fragrance of lily and light—breath of joy and life. Dancing upon the stairs without care. They lead us on. Do you not feel it? A quickening within yourself?" N. W. Clerk said.

"I do, Clerk. We ascend these stairs more quickly indeed," Nicholas said rejoicing.

In fact, their step had quickened. With song and virtue filling their sail.

Finally, the three travelers reached the top of the mountain and beheld the entrance to the castle. Unlike most castles that many imagine, a thick defensive door was absent. Nicholas thought there would be no need if there were no enemies. There was a long pathway paved with stone that led to the entrance. The entrance was as high as a cathedral and just as ornate. It was arched at the top. And all around the entrance were statues of many people. Some holding books, others kneeling, still others with a peaceful look on their face though their heart was pierced. There was one with lance in hand riding a horse, piercing a dragon through the mouth. Another of an angel holding a man down with his foot while pointing a sword at the man's face. The angel's face determined and at peace knowing what he had to do. Nicholas recognized the latter two as St. George and St. Michael from classical paintings and icons. There were a multitude of other saints, Nicholas gathered, carved around the colossal entrance.

As they walked past the entrance, before them was a long passage and to the left and right were thousands of people standing. They were not solemn, but joyful. Smiles and joy and life radiated from their countenances. It was not the solemnity of church nor the stern respect of a kingly court. Though deference and laud and respect and fealty was in the air. They were in a kingly court. The interior was gothic, white stone. A throne was at the end of the passageway. Gilt in gold. Marble leading up to the throne, and upon the throne was the King. In kingly raiment—red robe, with blue threaded throughout. He stood, a crown upon his head.

His voice boomed in welcome, "They have come. Now dress them aptly that they may approach me to receive their gift." At the King's word, attendants helped Nicholas and Clerk undress and redress. There was neither embarrassment nor lewdness. There was only joy to be taken out of the rags they wore, as Clerk considered his clothes. Nicholas didn't consider his clothes rags, but when they were removed he felt freed as though what he wore was a hindrance rather than a compliment to his form. His vanity was stripped away. Contentment filled his being. Then they were robed in white. The cloth was cotton and dazzlingly white. Nicholas could only think of purity. White as snow. The attendants pushed them on. Nicholas and Clerk walked toward the King standing before his throne. Nicholas looked back for Rigel, but he didn't see him.

But he saw the three ladies dressed in gossamer white with a tinge of blue with flower tiaras upon their heads who ran toward Nicholas. They were the same who passed them on the stairs ascending. Their beings light and free. Two kissed him upon his forehead and the last embraced him, leaving a fragrance of lily as she danced away from him. The two ladies with golden hair, the other with brown hair kissed by sunlight, skipped and danced down the hall toward the King. They smiled, radiating joy and laughed mellifluously. As they processed down the marble hall, they whirled like dryads on a spring day, scattering flower petals along the way. They reached the step before the King's throne, curtsied and moved to the left of the King and his throne.

Nicholas looked around him again. There were a multitude of people. Many had the likeness of images he had seen in books of the depiction of saints, plus many more he had never seen before.

A chorus of song filled the room. Each person sang with their whole heart.

Near the King sat a woman crowned with silver that was be-jeweled with diamonds. Her face was similar to the King's. She was robed in a soft blue and her veil covered the back of her head, the crown atop the veil. She sang, but also looked intently at Nicholas. She looked at him knowingly, a smile upon her lips. Nicholas rec-ognized her. The song echoed through the vestibule and through-out the castle that was more indicative of a cathedral in Nicholas' mind. As the chorus was sung, presences appeared in great flashes and bursts of light. They flitted through the cathedral ceiling and alighted amidst the people and behind the King's throne.

Nicholas smiled at Clerk. Clerk smiled back. They approached the throne of judgment that Rigel sang about in the psalm. Sud-denly, a great pressure surrounded Nicholas. He fell to the ground. Clerk stopped to help him up. Nicholas leant upon Clerk as they approached the King. The pressure subsided slightly, but Nicholas' head pounded with pain. They were finally before the King. They knelt before him—it seemed the right thing to do. Nicholas' head still swam, some of the pain dissipated.

"Rise, my children. Clive, step forward," the King said with music in his voice.

N. W. Clerk stepped forward. The King laid his hand upon his head for a moment. Then he handed Clerk a white stone. The King spoke to Clerk for some time, but Nicholas could not hear what was said. When Clerk turned to step down from the King, his forehead glistened and tears streamed his cheeks. His face beamed with joy. He, again, stood next to Nicholas.

"Nicholas, step forward, my child," the King said.

Nicholas stepped forward with minor stumbling. The pain in his head throbbed, only subsiding slightly. Once Nicholas was standing in front of the King, he put his hand upon Nicholas' head.

"Your mind knows many things. But in this place, it has been smashed, in a sense. What you knew is good. But you know its full-ness now. All wisdom comes from the King. In this land, you have come to see more fully." The King breathed on Nicholas' forehead.

"Your mind is healed. Receive the wisdom of the ages from the beginning. The breath of truth." Nicholas' head ceased to be in pain.

When the King removed his hand, Nicholas noticed a wound in the King's hand. Recognition dawned upon Nicholas. "You're the same man I met in the cave and in the Upper Room. How do you . . . how are you . . ."

"In all places? That is a mystery. I am the same and slightly different, all in all, but not confined to one thing. But let us not speak of such things. This matters not, at this present. Let me give you something." The King handed Nicholas a white stone. "Keep this with you always. For on the Last Day, you will see what is hidden upon it. It is but a white stone now, but on that day, you will see what is written upon the stone." The King then handed Nicholas a book. "Read this daily. But also write in this book often. See to the mark."

Nicholas put the white stone in a pocket on the left side of his white robe. Nicholas then opened the book where a bookmark divided the written portion from the blank pages. The first page said: journal of a wayfarer. The cloth bookmark had something written upon it. Nicholas read:

> *Sing in me, Lord, and through me tell the story*
> *Of ancient paths of heraldry,*
> *Honor, fortitude, fealty to the King.*
>
> *Oh, knights of old,*
> *Lord of beginnings and endings,*
> *Guard my heart and*
> *Commission me truth's wings*
> *To soar on winds of grace and mercy.*
> *On matters of truth, romance and chivalry.*
>
> *Oh maidens, hearts as strong fortresses;*
> *Outer mien—tall spires—*
> *Treasures, persuasion, pride, love within:*
> *Maidens: stately women, feminine, meek,*
> *Yet strong and true.*
>
> *Give me air of truth*

To say your story well.
Through me, Lord, speak truth in the
Hearts who read:
What men and women should be.

"Write your story. From this land and onward. Your name is in the book of life, but be cautious when you return to your own time. For the way is treacherous where cunning and craft can confuse."

The woman in blue with silver crown stood and moved toward Nicholas. Her blue robe shimmered silver and was edged with silver. She embraced him and kissed him upon his forehead.

She spoke, "Emmanuel, favored one. Do not be afraid. Nothing is impossible with the Holy One. For I have walked amidst the impossible. Listen to the King. He is the most wise and to be trusted. Do not be afraid. The King's love for you is beyond all that you can imagine."

"Thank you, my lady," Nicholas whispered.

The King smiled, his eyes composed, glistening with compassion. "Go to your beloved. Forgive her. The words in the book I have given you will give you fortitude, but also pray for courage. In time, she will forgive you. In time you will drink the wine of laughter and joy again. Remember that I exact perfect justice, but also perfect love. Let joviality fill your hearts. The red color of the cloth bookmark will remind you. Allow love to fill your hearts again. Not the love that wears out like a garment, but the love that endures that no flood can quench. Giving all to the other. For it is all of you that I ask of you. Giving your entire self, this will mend your broken heart. For it is in giving yourself that you are redeemed. You cannot give yourself life, she cannot either, and neither can anyone else. Only I can do this. If this rings true within you, kneel, and I will give you my blessing."

Nicholas kneeled before the King. The King said, "Before me kneels a man after my own heart. He has sought the truth, he has sought wisdom of man and of God. One has led him bereft of joy and peace. The other has brought him suffering. But a suffering that is redeemed. Only One has redeemed suffering and made it full of meaning. Your suffering has led you on a meandering path which has led you home. The journey has caused humility to grow within your heart. Your heart had been cold and hardened. But the heat of divine love has thawed it and caused it to bloom into life and joy. Frost and ice no more. Saturn's imaginative vigor reversed. Faith and hope have kissed your forehead and love has embraced you. You once worshiped idols and placed them in the high places. But they have been destroyed, smashed. In their place only One remains.

"In the strength of the King, you must return. Depart in peace, for I will go before you clearing the way. Ask for guidance and you will receive it. Ask for wisdom and the same will be given. Give what is given you. Rise, my child."

Nicholas rose. "How do I return?"

The King smiled and laughed. "Clive . . . sorry, Clerk, will lead you to the forest. He will lead you to the great oak. You will return there."

Nicholas turned to leave.

"But wait, take this ring with you." The King handed Nicholas a simple golden ring. There seemed to be nothing special about it. "When you get to the great oak. Put the ring on. It will help you in the return journey. Remember, this world as well as yours is God's. Leave here in joy and return in joy. My peace I leave with you."

"Thank you, your majesty. I will never forget this place. I will not forget you and all whom I have met along the way. I hope one day that I may return," Nicholas said.

"You will. I will see to it. Now go, you are needed in your hometown."

Nicholas bowed slightly before the King and the Lady in blue and silver and turned to leave with Clerk.

Chapter 12

The two, still robed in white, were directed to the left where a door opened to a stone pathway, which led into thick, green woods. Nicholas clenched the ring in his hand. He looked into the firmament above him to take in the nearness of the planets for the last time. He set his vision on Jupiter, large, red with orange and white mixtures. He stared at Jupiter's red wound in its side, the ever-present hurricane science has determined it to be. The king of planets, wounded, yet still sovereign.

N. W. Clerk and Nicholas walked across the stone pathway and into the lawn surrounded by trees. At the end of the lawn was a green-stone gazebo. It was weather-worn with moss growing on the stone. Nicholas picked at the moss. Both men looked at the forest surrounding them. The trees were large. Some trunks as wide as large doorways others as wide as small houses. Some shot straight into the sky. Others, many limbed, twisted to heights, like a large walking stick tree, limbs twisting and gnarled. Others had enormous limbs, one resting on the ground like an elephant trunk.

"Look at these trees," Nicholas said, "timeless, large, steadfast. Always growing, reaching. What wisdom they speak, living through many ages. Providing warmth and fuel, if felled. A canopy covering and protecting."

Beyond the gazebo, Nicholas spied a trail amidst the trees. Someone walked from the forest.

It was Rigel.

Nicholas rushed over to Rigel. "I'm glad you are here. You have been an excellent guide for me through this land. You even led me when I thought I was alone. Will you come with us to the great oak?"

"I will not go with you. I have come to say farewell."

Nicholas lowered his head in sorrow.

"But do not be saddened. You will see me in your world as well. Just look to the sky. I will be with you always. It was an honor to journey with you here."

"Thank you, Rigel. I suppose I cannot call upon you where I am returning to, only gaze upon your celestial state," Nicholas said.

"Oh, but you can. You just won't see me as you see me now. Not until you return to this land. In time you will. In time. You must not tarry here for long. The King has sent you back. I bid you farewell. But we will meet again," Rigel said.

"Yes, we must go. I cannot thank you enough. But yes, I will remember what you said. We will meet again," Nicholas said. He wanted to shake Rigel's hand, but that seemed too pedestrian. So he slightly bowed his head in honor.

"You give me honor and I thank you. Remember to also give all honor to the King. For I am but a servant. Now go with my blessing and the King's," Rigel said.

"Shall we go on?" Clerk said.

The two walked into the forest following the trail. It was a level dirt path. Ferns and mushrooms grew on either side of the path. After a time, the two travelers walked through a group of pines standing tall and straight. The wind rushed through the pines, quickening their step. The rushing was exhilarating, a quickening of the heart, as though joy flew by and rested within Nicholas and also flew past to find another mark. Through the soft, brown pine needles they went. The trail descended at this point, just past the pine grove. There was a gurgling sound ahead. The travelers came to a stream in the forest and a bridge made of logs. They crossed the bridge, but stopped in the middle to gaze at the water flowing by. In the water Nicholas saw small creatures swimming about. Other creatures jumped out of the water, causing small splashes as they landed in the water again. They weren't quite fish, but like fish, only more colorful and shimmered in the light that leaked through the green leaves above.

They moved forward, alighting upon the path again. This time they ascended again through a grove of beech trees. It was a long deep wood of them. Their bark curling off the trunk. A blue, red, and purple hue permeated the scene. There were floating white light orbs flickering. It almost looked like a wintery scape, except the air was warm and the leaves were still on the trees. As Clerk and Nicholas walked through the grove and passed the orbs, they heard a melody, which, as they passed, other orbs created a harmony—together a beautiful symphony. The scene was a beautiful display of sound and color. A harmonious delight. Nicholas didn't want to leave, but Clerk pushed him on.

They reached an even path again, no longer ascending. They came upon a field filled with wild flowers. The flowers were mostly red, but some blue and purple were scattered about. The temperature was cooler here. At the far end of the field was a large oak tree. When Nicholas looked at it a certain way, he saw the tree aglow with a golden light. But then he looked at it straight on and it was a normal oak tree at the end of a field. They walked toward the oak tree. Nicholas held his hands out allowing the flowers to play along his palms. Above there was a clearing. The sky was blue, the golden light had dimmed somewhat. It was nearing dusk. Prominent in the sky was Saturn with his rings.

Finally, the travelers were in front of the great oak. Its leaves dark and green. Limbs sturdy and strong. The trunk, a sentinel seeing all the ages of the world pass.

"Now what do I do?" Nicholas said.

"We wait. Oh, put the ring on," Clerk said.

Nicholas put the ring on. At that moment, the ground began to shake. The sky was growing dimmer, nearer to dusk. The tree turned from dark and strong to a golden shimmering. A way opened within the oak. It was like a pool, an undulating mirror looking upon another world. He saw the lamp-lit streets of his hometown. And the fountain at Belle Grove Park. It was still evening there.

"I suppose this is my moment of departure. It was a delight and an honor meeting you. Thank you for your wisdom and friendship. We will meet again, yes?" Nicholas said.

"Yes, indeed. For Christians never say good-bye." The two embraced. And then Nicholas walked through the undulating mirror. He felt a sensation of intense heat, like being within molten glass. But the pain subsided instantly, and he was in the cool of the evening at the fountain of Belle Grove Park. He looked into the sky. The stars twinkled in the atmosphere. The moon, pale and bright with Venus, blue and brilliant slightly below. Mars, red and severe slightly below Venus. And Jupiter was also prominent and luminous. (All great distances away, of course.) Nicholas' heart was free and full: of joy and peace. A contentment rested upon him.

He looked down at himself. He was no longer in the white robe, but in his regular clothes. The ring on his finger; he felt the book and white stone in his left pocket.

"I never did get any answer if I was in another world or another dimension or this world at the culmination. I think being there was the answer itself," Nicholas said aloud to no one in particular.

He walked toward Bond Street. Then passed Oak Street where oaks used to stand like pillars, holding the ground in place, supporting the sky. But now, those ancient sentinels, torn from the supple ground. But he could see the old sentinels standing strong and tall. One day they would be there again. He then passed Westmoreland Street, remembering his friend Tom. He didn't know where he was, but he sent a prayer heavenward, like incense rising.

There was a fragrance in the air. It was smoky and sweet. A holy smell. He breathed in the crisp, scented air. He almost wanted to dance, but he didn't know how. But his heart danced within him. Finally, he reached the lamppost that stood at the far end of his driveway. He went up to his front door and opened the door.

"I'm home," Nicholas said.

"You're home late," his wife said. They stood near each other. She held out her hands, he put his hands in hers. "I see you're wearing it again."

"What?"

"Your wedding ring," his wife said.

"Oh, right. Yes. I am."

They smiled at each other. Then embraced.

"We have a lot of work to do," Nicholas said. "And I have much to tell you."

The moon slipped behind a cumulus sailing across dark skies. The time for contemplation in isolation was over. It was a time to rekindle wonder and delight in their lives.

Appendix

HEAVEN BY EARTH'S DOOR

Enter the temple; enter heaven.

We are taken to the Holy of Holies.
We take; we eat,
bread and wine
not as simple as they seem,
They are in disguise.

The reality: Christ—
Dead, resurrected, seated at the Right.
The Great Cloud of Witnesses worship
And Celebrate in accord.

The trans-dimensional table
ravishes our Self to the Real.
The River of Life flowing forever
Sending like droplets
grace,
mercy,
forgiveness.

Where the sacrifice was made.
We ascending
In collusion to the High place
Offering ourselves
To be made
like Christ.

SOL

On the day of rest, Shabbat.
Oh! Solar flair
Cast thy wisdom upon darkened mind.
Liberality: Generosity in provision with prudent heart,
Love of knowledge for its own sake—seen a fool
To the pragmatist.
Solar wind grant wisdom to our hearts.
Wisdom—beloved of the true Sol—Pantocrater.
Bring thy light of wisdom to darkened soul,
That truth may be taught and shown with mercy.
Grace's wings alighting upon solar air.
With virtues' pinions on its wings.
Sol, slay the dragons within our hearts—those tempting, taunting.
Warm the day, let not Saturn's leaden frost steal the breath
which created all that is breathing.
With golden light guide mind and heart toward you—
Source of life.
Eternal one; holy and mighty
Brighten our day with wisdom's light—
Blossoming beauty, truth, goodness.
Terrible light, absolute,
Strike me down that I may be humbled.
Blinding light, life-giving
You abide not wickedness, yet show mercy.
I am in awe of you.

MERCURY

Swift of speed.
Causing all the gifts of Jupiter
Swift delivery
To all who carry breath.
Articulation and meaning
The importance of language and understanding.

Wisdom and breath strive mutually
Articulating meaning to a world that is blind.
Woden its day.

VENUS

Mistaken for the One True,
Tempted to worship the sweet embraces,
The silver caresses,
Of Eros' giddy return.
Love's laugh, echoes joy eternal.
Frivolity at week's end.
Her incense filling the atmosphere.
Springing life wherever she treads.
Greenery springing forth . . . dancing in the moonlight.
Breasts providing.
Luna and Jupiter guiding and ordering
Love's full and true purpose.

TERRA

Under rule of the enemy
All influences distorted.
Mars: used to murder.
Venus: used for lust.
Jupiter: for hubris.
Saturn: suicidal, destruction.
Mercury: confusion.
Luna: insanity.
Sol: pride in knowledge.
But Terra too, will be renewed.

LUNA

Monday her day.
Silver and water.
Paleness and beauty.
Water giving life to all who carry breath within them.
Lunacy a fallacy.
More a melancholy but a mirror to Sol.
Wisdom and melancholy tend to co-mingle.
Solomon knew this well.
Luna cause delight, water our souls with silver yearning to
Compliment Sol's gold.

MARS

Looking on with uncaring red-eye,
As nations war,
Inspiring martiality.
Yet all vegetation praises.
The harvest ripe
For eternal despair or eternal joy.
His hand strong; hard,
fist ready to strike.
Yet element of chivalry keeping barbarism at bay.
Tuesday his day.
Virtue lies in the bosom of Mars,
March his month birthing life in Spring.
Masculinity his game,
Not misogyny or arrogance,
But part of the image,
This martial spirit gives men
Strength to fight, not flesh and blood,
But power unseen, diabolic, demonic.
The hardened fist,
The sharpened spear,
All aimed at the foe of soul.

JUPITER

Kingly raiment, red and gold.
Red eye, seeing.
Jovial spirit, sending joy and mirth
to ungrateful mud.
Dust to dust, joviality and mirth temporary
until finding distraction in their own gold,
greed,
and lust.
Jupiter bleeds,
gaping red,
Gaping wound healing all the world—
Influence hovering over water and spirit.
God's finest creation looks on with uncaring eye.
Jupiter,
Jove worshiped, mistaken for the One True.
Humans' fickle heart
looks upon its inward cosmos,
neglecting the order of God's.
No longer looking outward,
man taking without gratitude.
Jupiter spins on its axis
speedily, silent.
Awaiting the Last Day,
when Jove will be glorified
with all of creation.
Eternal mirth,
eternal joy,
red with reverie,
we will be.
Joining in the dance
of the planetae.
Together with Jove regaled in kingly guise
with the One King of all,
we dance to perfect harmony—

the music of the spheres.
Thursday his day.

SATURN

Chin frosted with eternal winters bite.
The woes of men a delight
To the ringed planet.
Melancholy his game.
Weighted heart,
Of woe's desire.
Leaden weight plunged in darkness.
Living under the affliction of Saturn;
waiting for Jove, His glorious restoration—wrapping us in a cloak
of red splendor.
Yet, Saturn brings the Last Day.
A glory to see. For all glory will remain.

Waiting in the world
Between worlds.
Between sleeping and waking.
Where visions and becoming occur.

I wept a river—
Flowing through old rivulets,
Leading to the pool of Lethe.
Placed around my bed—lotus—
Drinking in fragrance of forgetfulness.

I had a terrible dream.

Numinous dread
Splintered all I was and am.

A shaft of light struck my countenance,
Piercing my heart.

He was made present.
I took the cup; drank.
A piece of flesh: eaten.
Washed in fire and blood.
Remembrance manifest.
I awoke,
reminiscence my drink.

Pieces lost each day
Time ticks away
Losing pieces of myself to the doldrums of the day.
Pieces of my flesh, sarx,
Drop in the memory of the day.
Blood bleeding
Seeping into the ground.
Dying.

Being, in the Presence of the omniscient
All of me falls to the ground.

I look at the stars in deep heaven
I remember pieces of me . . .
Deep in the ground.
The dew of Grace, manna from heaven
Nourish the lifeless pieces,
Bursting through in new life.

The Northern Cross embraces the sky
Curving earthward,
Reminding children of hope
The story of the god-man dying
to bring all the world
All the universe under Him
Into new life.

COSMIC DISSONANCE

The crescent moon
Smiling
Rising with the Pleaides.

A traveler upon the road
Walks with the stars.

Dust or a rock fragment
Burns through Earth's atmosphere.
The travelers heart watches and burns,
Streaking across the sky.

Ursa major and minor
Stomp on Leo, roaring lion.

Saturn and Mars blink down
Reflecting the Sun's light.
Mars burns red in the night
Tempting the traveler toward rebellion and war.
Saturn (Cronos), father creator, says,
"Look upon my splendor."

The morning star has set—a cold spot glows in the traveler's
heart.
Orion dips toward the horizon in the southern sky,
His dogs at his heels.
Taurus burns bright.
Orion has little hope of killing the fine beast.

The traveler moves ahead with the stories of the stars above.
Virgo, her light in the East whispers a prayer,
"Press on."

The seasons change with the stars.

Appendix

When the summer triangle rises,
What will have changed?
When Orion goes to rest,
How much will be added to the traveler's story?
When Bootes awakes,
Arcturus flickering orange,
Will the traveler be among Boote's flock?

Hercules, the bears, the King and Queen, and the Dragon always
know each season.
Timeless Lyra, strumming music of the stars—watches and prays.
David singing psalms in the quiet, wilderness of stars also
prays—"seek the face of God."

The traveler sees the reflection of the constellations and presses
on in the cosmos,
awaiting the Last Day in hope.
In the meantime, stars remind him of Time and Eternity.

All I need is a view of the Moon and Venus nestled nearby.
The sky brimming red and washing blue.
A calm lake in my view to enhance the fading of the blue.

The sliver Moon and starry Venus hold my eye
A longing breathes from me and I grasp a glimpse into heaven.
The distance pulled close for an instant.

A calming pond sits before me.
Its smooth surface beckoning me to be as placid.

The reflection of the sliver Moon and starry Venus—Still;
becalming my soul, my entire being.

Looking through
Wavering pane,
Upon green, tamed land.
The sidewalk snaking
Toward benches.

A solitary man crosses himself.

He raises his eyes to blue heavens
Holding his heavy burden in his hands,
Bent in supplication:
Creator and creature.

An exchange of love.
Deepening his will
Filling with grace and Agape.

As the sun says goodbye
In a pink and orange wash,
King and subject agree,
"My burden is easy,
My burden is light."

CREATION

Alpha, beginning,

is,

always.

Spirit hovering over the faceless void.

Nothing.

Spoken into being.

Light: particle and wave careening through space,

Darkness framing the universe.

Galaxies, Suns, elements, planets, gases all converging into the order of the Cosmos.

Music of the Spheres. Gravity holding order. The stars and planets, asteroids, mountains of dust serving the Creator and showing His majesty and glory. The music a symphony creating harmony and melody. The unseen and the seen. The light waves unseen make the perfect music of the cosmos.

God spoke and all visible and invisible was created. It was good.

The Earth created. Day and night (the moon to keep the planets wobble to a minimum and the Sun perfect distance to allow life). The sea and the land. The atmosphere to protect us from gamma rays, ultra violet rays, harmful radiation.

The plants and animals of the land and the sea. Moving in accordance with His word. Every act in praise to God.

Man: created in the Image and likeness of God. To be in union and submission to his Creator. Delighting in all that God has given him. Man's delight: praise and glory to God. Man companion to God and created order. Naming the animals and plants and all that is seen. Knowing the unseen. Though man loved all that God gave him, there was one companion amiss. God created woman. The image of God complete.

The embrace of love of the Three-person God

Burst forth the created order.

With planet, suns, galaxies,

Earth: with animals, plants

Man and woman as the culmination.

Relationship bursting forth love.

Eros, Agape.

Agape unconditional. Willing one thing. Purity of heart. He does not think of His own desire but that of the other.

All put in place to glorify the Creator and that the created may know the Creator.

Father: protector, lover, disciplinarian. Son: of the Father enacting all that is spoken. Spirit: power to create and instill Himself in creation. That we may be like Him and love like Him and have the Mind of Christ; the mind and power of God to be creative in His will to glorify Him that has given. To release the power of God who raised Christ from the dead. Who called nothing into being. His power in all, but not confined to any. God created for the good of all. He yearns for our return to know Him.

THE FALL

The garden walled, guarded all God created. A deceiver with forked tongue and conniving spirit distorted God's truth. Man fell. He wanted to judge for himself. Wanted authority. Usurpation of the high command. In our weakness, we decide what may be right and what may be wrong. We are Kings and Queens. God does not exist. We must be gods.

Yet, the moral Law exists. From the beginning. Since we fell over ourselves in our greed to take charge, God's graciousness and love for us has allowed us to know, to remember His Law.

However, we were banished from paradise. The flaming wall blocking the entrance. On our own we toil. The image marred. Some traces remain.

Satan and sin distorting the harmony of the cosmos. Pangaea breaks. Tectonic plates rent. Earthquakes, storms, hurricanes, tornadoes. Disobedience of men causes a disobedience of animals. The tame become wild. Some have a proclivity to become domestic. When God's promise was fulfilled, many wild animals have the potential for domestication.

The dangers of the outer cosmos do not harm our planet, though meteors hurtle close to the planet occasionally smashing down. Supernovas occur. Black holes devour. The universe thrown into upheaval. A war of the unseen battle affecting directly what is seen.

The fall, when sin entered the world, the universe, all of creation.

Sin affecting everything.

Starting the battle for the soul of mankind.

Chaos, disorder. An unraveling of the order.

Yet, the head of the serpent will be crushed by the seed of the woman.

Protoevangelium: the reality of all coming under the King. A renewal. Bright, burning light to overcome all evil, all distortion of the created order.

Sin has its day, but has its end in Christ the everlasting, giver of eternal life.